MAY 0 5

Millions of Americans remember Dick and Jane (and Sally and Spot too!). The little stories with their simple vocabulary words and warmly rendered illustrations were a hallmark of American education in the 1950s and 1960s.

But the first Dick and Jane stories actually appeared much earlier—in the Scott Foresman Elson Basic Reader Pre-Primer, copyright 1930. These books featured short, upbeat, and highly readable stories for children. The pages were filled with colorful characters and large, easy-to-read Century Schoolbook typeface. There were fun adventures around every corner of Dick and Jane's world.

Generations of American children learned to read with Dick and Jane, and many still cherish the memory of reading the simple stories on their own. Today, Pearson Scott Foresman remains committed to helping all children learn to read—and love to read. As part of Pearson Education, the world's largest educational publisher, Pearson Scott Foresman is honored to reissue these classic Dick and Jane stories, with Grosset & Dunlap, a division of Penguin Young Readers Group. Reading has always been at the heart of everything we do, and we sincerely hope that reading is an important part of your life too.

Dick and Jane is a registered trademark of Addison-Wesley Educational Publishers, Inc.
From THE NEW WE LOOK AND SEE. Copyright © 1956 by Scott, Foresman and Company,
copyright renewed 1984. From WE READ PICTURES. Copyright © 1951 by Scott, Foresman
and Company, copyright renewed 1979. From WE READ MORE PICTURES. Copyright © 1951
by Scott, Foresman and Company, copyright renewed 1979. From THE NEW WE COME
AND GO. Copyright © 1956 by Scott, Foresman and Company, copyright renewed 1984.
All rights reserved. Published in 2004 by Grosset & Dunlap, a division of Penguin Young
Readers Group, 345 Hudson Street, New York, NY, 10014. GROSSET & DUNLAP is a
trademark of Penguin Group (USA) Inc. Published simultaneously in Canada.
Printed in the U.S.A.

Library of Congress Cataloging-in-Publication Data
Away we go.
    p. cm. — (Read with Dick and Jane ; 7)
    Summary: A collection of classic Dick and Jane stories in which they play with Sally, Tim,
Spot, and Puff, and take a trip with their parents.
    ISBN 0-448-43406-7 (pbk.) — ISBN 0-448-43492-X (hardcover)
    [1. Play—Fiction. 2. Pets—Fiction. 3. Automobile travel—Fiction. 4. Vocabulary.] I. Series.
PZ7.A96114 2004
[E]—dc22   2003016827

ISBN 0-448-43492-X (GB)   A B C D E F G H I J
ISBN 0-448-43406-7 (pbk)   A B C D E F G H I J

Read with
Dick and Jane

Away We Go

GROSSET & DUNLAP • NEW YORK

Tim

Jump up, Sally.

Jump up.

Come, Sally.

Jump up.

Jump up, Tim.

Jump up.

Up, up, up.

Jump up.

Look, Dick.

See Sally and Tim.

Funny, funny Sally.

Funny, funny Tim.

Tim and Spot

Go, Tim.

Go up.

Go up, Tim.

Go up, up, up.

Go, Tim.

Go down.

Go, go, go.

Go down.

Go down, down, down.

Oh, Jane.

See Spot and Tim.

See Spot run.

See funny Spot.

See funny Tim.

Up, Tim

Up Puff, up.
Come Puff, come.

Oh, oh.

See Puff jump down.

Up Puff, up.
Jump up, Puff.
Jump up.

See Tim.

Up, Tim, up.

Run Away Spot

"Oh, Spot," said Jane.
"You can not play here."

Jane said, "I can make a house."

"I can make a little house,"
said Jane.

"Down comes my house," said Jane.
"Down it comes.
Run away, Spot.
You can not play here."

Down It Comes

Dick said, "I can make a house.
A big house for two boats.
A house for the yellow boat.
And for the blue boat.
See my big house."

Jane said, "I can make a house.
A big house for three cars.
Red and blue and yellow cars."

Sally said, "I can make a house.

A little house for Tim.

Here is my house for Tim.

Tim is in it.

Tim can play in it.

Oh, oh, oh.

Tim looks funny in the house."

"See my house," said Dick.
"Down it comes."

"See my house," said Jane.
"Down, down it comes."

"Oh, oh, oh," said Sally.
"Down comes my little house.
Run away, Puff.
Run away, Spot.
You can not play here."

Away We Go

Sally said, "Away we go.
Away we go in the car.
Mother and Father.
Dick and Jane.
Sally and Tim."

Dick said, "Spot is not here.
Puff is not here."

Dick said, "I see something.

Look down, Jane.

Look down and see something.

It is funny.

Can you see it?"

"Oh, oh," said Jane.

"Here is Spot."

"Come in, Spot," said Jane.
"You can go in the car."

"Away we go," said Sally.
"Away we go in the car.
Mother and Father.
Dick and Jane.
Sally and Tim and Spot.
Away we go in the big, big car."

See It Go

Jane said, "Look, look.
I see a big yellow car.
See the yellow car go."

Sally said, "I see it.
I see the big yellow car.
I want to go away in it.
I want to go away, away."

Dick said, "Look up, Sally.
You can see something.
It is red and yellow.
It can go up, up, up.
It can go away."

Sally said, "I want to go up.
I want to go up in it.
I want to go up, up, up.
I want to go up and away."

"Look, Sally," said Dick.
"Here is Father in a boat.
You can go away in it."

"Jump in, jump in," said Father.
"Jump in the big blue boat."

"We can go," said Sally.
"We can go away in the boat.
Away in a big blue boat."